MOMMY GOOSE

GOOSE

Rhymes from the Mountains

MIKE NORRIS   *Carved illustrations by* MINNIE ADKINS

UNIVERSITY PRESS OF KENTUCKY

Copyright © 2016 by The University Press of Kentucky

Scholarly publisher for the Commonwealth,
serving Bellarmine University, Berea College, Centre
College of Kentucky, Eastern Kentucky University,
The Filson Historical Society, Georgetown College,
Kentucky Historical Society, Kentucky State University,
Morehead State University, Murray State University,
Northern Kentucky University, Transylvania University,
University of Kentucky, University of Louisville,
and Western Kentucky University.
All rights reserved.

Editorial and Sales Offices: The University Press of Kentucky
663 South Limestone Street, Lexington, Kentucky 40508-4008
www.kentuckypress.com

Cataloging-in-Publication data is available from the Library of Congress.

ISBN 978-0-8131-6614-8 (hardcover : alk. paper)
ISBN 978-0-8131-6687-2 (pdf)

This book is printed on acid-free paper meeting
the requirements of the American National Standard
for Permanence in Paper for Printed Library Materials.

Manufactured in South Korea.
Production location: WE SP, Paju-Si, South Korea
Date of Production: 8/26/2015
Cohort: Batch 1

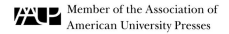 Member of the Association of
American University Presses

front cover: Vintage Oval Frame Photo
© RedDaxLuma | Dreamstime.com.
Photography and page design by Mike Norris.
Design and production assistance by BW&A Books, Inc.

To Carmen; Cari; John; Samuel; Noemi; Granta Martin;
Mother; and Centre College, which, though I never
attended, provided me with an education
   —*Mike Norris*

To the memory of my wonderful parents, John and Mona
Wooldridge; brothers June and Edgar; and sister Evelyn
   —*Minnie Adkins*

Special thanks to Greg Adkins, Mike Adkins,
Larry Bitensky, Sharon Boggs, Chris Floyd,
Bob Gottlieb, David Newton, Michael Startzman,
Randy Wilson, Sean Wright, and—for their singing
on the recording of "Tell Me, Mommy Goose"—
regulars of the Lexington Senior Citizens Center
and the first-grade classes at Carr Creek
Elementary School

Contents

EXTRA EGGS

When you listen to Mommy Goose,
You may forget the words she said,
  but forty years later they're still in your head.
In your heart and on your tongue,
  you'll be in the hills and young.
Listen to Mommy Goose.

Without knowing the force of words,
it is impossible to know more.

—*Confucius*

About
MOMMY GOOSE

Mommy Goose is an Appalachian bird.
Like cows love corn, she loves words.
She says,
"Corn can be yellow, blue, or white,
And words change colors in different light.
To talk like your flock is no disgrace.
Just use the right word in the right place."

Hammer and Nail

"Crack, crack, crack."
The hammer said that,
As he hit the nail three times.

The nail said, "Owww,
You're in trouble now.
I'll law you for this crime."

3

The Raccoons

The raccoons ate up all our corn,
Climbed in the car and honked the horn.

They played the radio and danced,

And tried on Granpaw's
underpants.

5

With handy hands like me and you,
There's not a lot they can't do.

If how it goes is how it went,
They'll own the place,
and we'll pay rent.

6

Old Doc Hale

Old Doc Hale went to jail,
For buying his papers through the mail.
He used a rope for a stethoscope,
And gave shots with a #9 nail.

Calico Cat

Big and fat,
The calico cat
Slept through his dinner.
Now full of sorrow,
He'll wait till tomorrow,
When he's a little thinner.

A WORD CAN be SOUR,
OR SWEET AS A KISS,
SofT as a PuRR,
HARSh as a hiss!

Level Cows

Granpaw's farm is hilly land,
With no smooth place
    for the cows to stand;
But they stay level
    as a croquet court,
Two legs long, and
    two legs short.

Little Mary

Little Mary wouldn't mind,
And said things to sister that were unkind.

She'd stomp her feet and hold her breath,
And scare her mommy half to death.

She grew up and had twin girls,
With big blue eyes and yellow curls.
They were sweet and cute at first,

Then acted just like her, but worse.

Speckled Hen

At quarter to ten,
The speckled hen,
Laid an egg
    with a double yolk.

She danced around,
Then ran to town,
Carrying it in a poke.

14

Mommy Fell

When Mommy fell out of the apple tree,
She got right up and went on a spree.
She danced a jig on the featherbed,
Then baked two bushels of gingerbread.
She used our tablecloth for a cape,
And made a necklace with measuring tape.
She tried to crochet with her feet,
Way up in the night before she fell asleep.

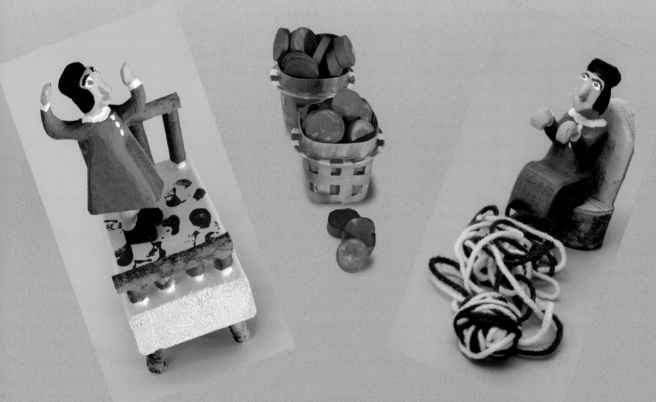

She stomped in the kitchen next morning and said,
"Who tracked mud all over my bed?
Why, look at the floor, covered with crumbs.
And where did all this gingerbread come from?
I don't know who I have to thank
For being so pyert as to pull such a prank,

But I'll find out before
the day's through,
And they'll be in big trouble
when I do!"

Lester Frye

Lester Frye was bad to lie.
You couldn't believe a word he said.
When he hollered, "Come back,
It's a heart attack,"
They laughed and went on to bed.

Mommy Had to Mop

The kitchen was dirty.
Mommy had to mop.
She cleaned every crumb.
She wouldn't stop.
Then she sat at the table,
And drunk her a pop.

Some words strike home.
Some are glancing.
Some make you moan.
Some set you dancing.

Lizzie Green

Lizzie Green was long and lean.
All the boys treated her mean.
She petted a possum.
Her beauty blossomed.
The county crowned her
    May Day queen.

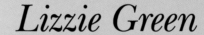

Billy Was Bad

Billy was bad, but wouldn't lie.
Teacher said, "Now look me in the eye.
You took toys that weren't yours,
And tied tin cans to the cat.
Aren't you ashamed to look in the mirror,
And see such a naughty boy as that?"

"Those old toys were just painted wood,
And all that running prob'ly
did the cat good.
I'm not sorry I was naughty,
I feel sorry because you caught me."

Rooster Can't Crow

Littlety low,
And cocklety coop,
The rooster can't crow,
He's down with the croup.

Blickery blust,
And slickery sloop,
There's no eggs for breakfast,
We'll have to eat soup.

Aunt Sal

Aunt Sal invited
    a slew to supper,
And dressed for the guests
In her best bib and tucker.
But the beans boiled dry,
And the dog ate chess pie,
While she primped
    in front of the mirror.

Little Johnny Hicks

Little Johnny Hicks
  was mighty sick.
The doctor thought him dead.
But Granmaw's cooking
  did the trick:
Soup beans and corn bread.

A WORD iS THE BRICK,
THAT BuildS THE BooK.
IT CAN be JUST THE TRICK,
oR GobbLedYgooK.

The Kudzu Man

The Kudzu Man is dead asleep,
But soon he'll stir, and move his feet.
His skin will turn to green from brown,
As his fingers reach along the ground,
Down the hill and around the pond,
Under the fence and over the barn.

He shakes his head
   to see how he's paid,
Squirted with poison,
   cut with blades.
What kind of crime could
   make them so vexed?
He just loves sunshine
   and seeing what's next.

The Rooster

The rooster started pecking
  at Granpaw's legs,
Then tried to flog Granmaw
  as she gathered eggs.
Granmaw boiled water,
While I churned butter.
That night we had
  fried chicken for supper.

Wake Up, Girls

Wake up, girls,
Your golden curls
Will go uncombed today.
The rooster's dead.
We laid in bed.
They'll dock us
  half our pay.

The Bluebird and Robin

The bluebird stole a robin's heart,
And tied it down with a double knot.
She sang him songs and called him darling.
Then flew away with a starling.

25

The June Bug

The June bug complained to the ant,
"My get up and go has got up and went."
"Sorry," said the ant,
    "but we must remember,
You *are* a June bug,
    and it *is* September."

A WORD CAN be boRiNg.
A WORD CAN be News.
A WORD'S Always WAiTiNg
FOR YOU TO Choose.

26

Fiddle It High

Fiddle it high, fiddle it low,
Fiddle it back around.
Fiddle till you break the bow,
And the stars all fall down.

Extra Eggs

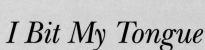

Benjamin Grimes

Benjamin Grimes
Went down in the mines,
But only lasted three days.
The note from the clerk
Said, "Unwilling to work,"
But Ben said it wasn't that way.

"Had nary a trouble
With pick or shovel,
Till something come up grey.
Not a loafer or shirker,
But one thing for certain,
I'd druther draw breath than pay."

I Bit My Tongue

I bit my tongue,
    and now it's sore.
I hope I don't bite
    my tongue no more.

Pray for the Pot

Pray for the pot.
Pray for the pot.
Sometimes
    it's full,
Sometimes
    it's not.

The Boy from Rowdy

A boy lived way back in Rowdy,
Who hated to tell people howdy.
He'd frown at the ground,
Make nary a sound,
And walk away looking pouty.

Possum and Bear

Though her house was a fixer-upper,
The possum invited the bear to supper.
She laid her table with Queen Anne's lace,
And a Red Rock bottle made a vase.
She served beans and greens
    and pickled beets,
And for dessert, sweet potato treats.

"How was it?" she asked, lowering her eyes.
 He smiled and made this reply:
"You've completely satisfied my hunger.
 I wish we'd met when I was younger."

Penny in the Well

I threw a penny in the well,
To see what secrets it would tell.
"Say, what will one penny buy
To know the future surer?"

"If you let another fly,
You'll be two pennies poorer."

Uncle Ed

Everybody said Uncle Ed
Could really pick the guitar.

But when we'd ask him to play,
He'd always say,
Maybe he might would tomorrow.

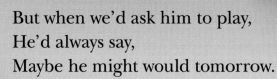

Cow's in the Barn

Cow's in the barn.
Kitten's in the yarn.
Daddy's in Harlan,
Bending his arm.

Love Me, Love You

Love me, love you,
Kiss and coo,
I hope we don't fall out.
If you break my heart,
I'll break yours too,
And that'll be turn about.

I Know an Old Man

I know an old man with a crusty nose.
The more it runs, the harder he blows.
He carries a funnel to help him hear,
And braids the hair growing out of his ears.
He walks into town twitching his tongue,
And flicks his teeth in and out just for fun.

Nag, Nag, Nag

"Nag, nag, nag, it never stops."

"Why don't you mend the door?"

"I'll oil the hinges and the lock,
And never come back no more."

Clete, the Parakeet

Clete, the parakeet, could talk up a storm.
He'd say, "I'll take a taste. What's the harm?"
Then he'd dance and shake his head,
And scream, "Done wore out. Ready for bed."
All day long till company came.
Then he'd limp like he was lame.
We'd beg him to say all the things he said,
But he'd fly to the perch and hide his head.
Soon as they left, he'd let out a squawk,
And yell, "I don't believe that bird can talk."

Daddy Hammered

When Daddy missed the nail,
And hammered his finger,
He turned right pale,
Then squalled like a painter.

Harlie Creech

Harlie Creech was over neat.
He swept the house morning and night.
He ironed his socks and starched his sheets,
And used a yardstick to get the quilts right.
South down the road lived Mildred Mays,
And in that direction Harlie would gaze.
Her hair was perfect, her shoes shined slick,
But Harley hesitated, suspecting a trick.
Who knew what horrors lay in store,
Rumpled pillows, crumbs on the floor?
At last his love made him risk the ordeal,
And Harlie invited her for a meal.
He scrubbed the house once, then again.
With trembling hand he welcomed her in.

Then Harlie froze and held his breath,
As Mildred Mays passed the test:
She took one look and said,
"This place is a mess."

The Latch and Keep

"Look at me," said the latch, "how I roll and spin.
I control this cab'net, what goes out and in,
While you, you keep, on the side of the case,
Hang flat and frozen in the same place."
The keep kept still and stared ahead.
Whatever she thought remained unsaid.
"A keep," cried the latch, "is boring at best,
Unable to move, forever at rest.
Your luck's to be stuck while I can fly.
You'll never match me . . . no need to try."

The keep, still staring, made this reply:

"You sway back and forth, leaning and preening,
It's true, you move, but without meaning.
I own I stay still while you whirl and swing,
But we're two parts of the same thing.
You wind around like the hands of a clock,
But I'm the one who orders, 'Stop!'
Alone, you lack reason and rule.
A latch that can't keep is a spinning fool."
The latch slowed down and made a stiff face,
And with one last turn, he locked into place.

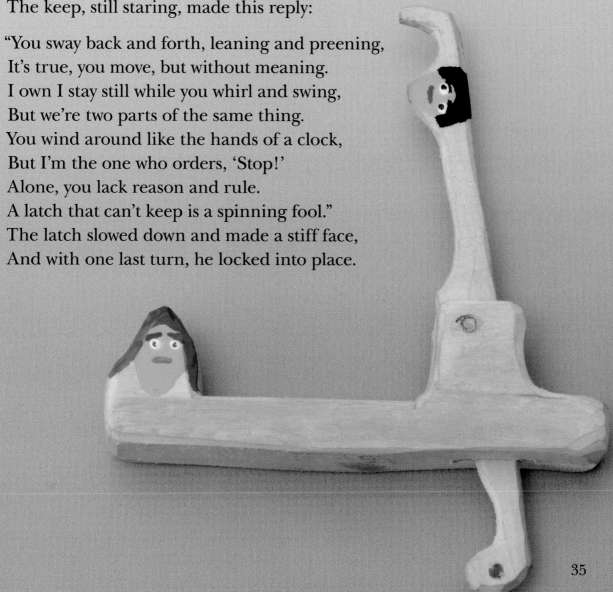

35

Kite

Would you like
   to fly a kite?
Be sure to get the
   tail on right.
And careful how
   you tie the string,
Or you won't be
   flying anything.
If the wind is weak
   overhead,
We'll bake gingerbread
   instead.

Who, Who, Who?

"Who, who, who?"
   said the hooty owl.
"Who do you think?"
   said I.
"You and me
   and a bumblebee,
And the moon
   up in the sky."

The Prettiest Sight

The prettiest sight
   I ever saw,
Was the backside
   of your head,
As you walked away
   to tell John Gray,
You'd chosen me
   instead.

Blind Sam Young

Blind Sam Young had a silver tongue,
And charged for his time.
He'd say, "Sad or funny,
For a piece of your money,
And two cents extra for rhyme."

The Road

Uncle Lew's road got paved.
He wouldn't say
   how much he paid.

Spring

Winter's over.
   It should be warm,
But the wind makes
   goosebumps on my arm.
We start a game.
   I run and hide,
But before they find me,
   I slip inside.
The sun is shining,
   but his rays are weak.
Warm has won
   at hide and seek.
Winter chill
   claims to be king,
But the coldest cold is in the spring.

I POUR OUT OF a BOTTOMLESS CUP,
NAME ME
SWEET, BITTER, RoUgh, ANd TENdER,
TASTEd ANd WaStED,
NEVER USEd UP.

A Word from Mommy Goose

A word can be kind.
A word can be mean.
A word can turn you red,
Or green.

A word makes it deep.
A word makes it light.
A word can make peace,
Or spark a fight.

Anything that strong
Is good for a friend.
A word started this story,
And a word is

the end.

Tell Me, Mommy Goose

Mike Norris
Transcribed by David Newton

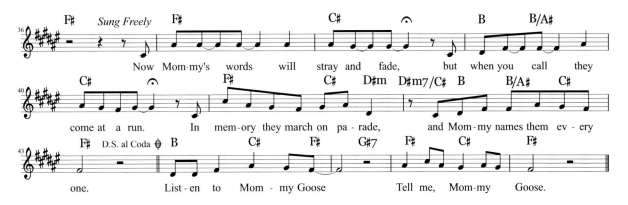

Now Mom-my's words will stray and fade, but when you call they come at a run. In mem-ory they march on pa - rade, and Mom-my names them ev - ery one. List - en to Mom - my Goose Tell me, Mom-my Goose.

Additional lyrics

Why Aunt Sal burned the beans, why the cat was looking lean,
The kudzu goes from brown to green, how Harlie thought his house was clean,
Tell me, tell me, tell me.

What it was Sam Young sold, how the coal dust took a toll,
Springtime is the coldest cold, how the words will grab ahold,
Tell me, tell me, tell me.

How the old man made a face, when Clete would beg to take a taste,
The table laid with Queen Anne's lace, and Daddy gone when we'd say grace,
Tell me, Mommy Goose.

Chorus

About the boy who bit his tongue, short and long the cows would come,
Mommy cleaning every crumb, and what she did when she got done,
Tell me, tell me, tell me.

How we pestered Uncle Ed, that night you chose me instead,
The bluebird doubled up her thread, and Johnny Hicks sat up in bed,
Tell me, tell me, tell me.

Cocklety coop, littlety low, Lizzie finally stole the show,
The boy who wouldn't say hello, how love passes to and fro,
Tell me, Mommy Goose.

Chorus

How the door was left behind, why feathers fall below the lines,
Two cents extra if it rhymes, what the hoot owl said three times,
Tell me, tell me, tell me.

How a kite climbs in the wind, the morning that the girls slept in,
Doc Hale drew five to ten, and how the rooster met his end,
Tell me, tell me, tell me.

So fiddle low, fiddle high, while the dog eats chess pie,
The speckled hen goes running by, what never is in short supply?
Tell me, Mommy Goose.

Coda and chorus, slowly. Complete song is intro, 12 verses with choruses, coda, and final
chorus sung slowly. (A recording is available for download at kentuckypress.com.)

About the Author and Illustrator

Mike Norris

A native of Eastern Kentucky, Mike Norris has been writing stories, poems, and songs for more than forty years. His songs have been recorded by country, folk, and bluegrass musicians. He recorded one album with the Raggedy Robin String Band and four albums of original music with the Americana group Billyblues. He worked for Centre College in the Communications Office for many years. He has written two other children's books, *Sonny the Monkey* and *Bright Blue Rooster,* and is the father of Cari and John Norris, also songwriters and musicians. He lives in Lexington, Kentucky, with his wife, Carmen.

Minnie Adkins

Minnie Adkins, who has been carving since she was five years old, is one of America's best-known folk artists. Among numerous honors, she has won the Folk Art Society of America Distinguished Artist Award, the Governor's Award for the Arts, the Centre College Norton Award, and the Morehead University Appalachian Treasure Award. Her work is part of many permanent collections, including those of the Smithsonian Museum; the National Gallery of Art in Washington, D.C.; the Huntington Museum of Art; and the Kentucky Folk Art Center. She has illustrated two other children's books, *Sonny the Monkey* and *Bright Blue Rooster,* and lives in Isonville, Kentucky.